THE LEPRECHAUN WHO WISHED HE WASN'T

'A *brilliant adventure story*' The Offaly Topic

Siobhán Parkinson

The author of several books for young readers, Siobhán lives in Dublin with her woodturner husband, Roger Bennett, and her personal nine-year-old proofreader, Matthew. Her primary interests are reading and writing, and she also sings in a choir (very quietly, in case she is found out!).

Her other books are:

Amelia
No Peace For Amelia
Sisters ... No Way!
Four Kids, Three Cats, Two Cows, One Witch (maybe)
The Moon King
All Shining In The Spring

All published by The O'Brien Press

The Leprechaun Who Wished He Wasn't

Siobhán Parkinson

Illustrated by
Donald Teskey

THE O'BRIEN PRESS
DUBLIN

First published 1993 by The O'Brien Press Ltd.,
20 Victoria Road, Dublin 6, Ireland
Tel. +353 1 4923333 Fax. +353 1 4922777
e-mail books@obrien.ie
Website http://www.obrien.ie
Reprinted 1994, 1997 (twice), 1999

5   6   7   8   9   10
99   00   01   02   03   04

British Library Cataloguing-in-publication Data
Parkinson, Siobhan
Leprechaun Who Wished He Wasn't
I Title II Teskey, Donald
823.914 [J]

ISBN 0-86278-334-8

The O'Brien Press receives
assistance from

The Arts Council
An Chomhairle Ealaíon

Editing, typesetting, design, layout: The O'Brien Press Ltd.
Cover illustration: Donald Teskey
Printing: Cox & Wyman Ltd., Reading

To my father

For 'Murricans' and Other Aliens

amadán: fool, idiot, half-wit (pronounced *omodhaun*)

báinín: a whitish (undyed) wool or woollen material, part of traditional Irish dress (pronounced *bawneen*)

begobs and begorrah: words that people *think* Irish people say

buachallán: ragwort. There is a folk tale about a leprechaun who buried his crock of gold under a *buachallán*, a very good hiding place, as every Irish meadow is full of them (pronounced *booakallaun*)

eejit: an Irish way of saying 'idiot'

ogham: a script consisting of small lines drawn at various angles to a central vertical line, used in ancient Ireland for marking runes on stones (pronounced *ogum*)

raiméis: rubbish, nonsense (pronounced *rawmaysh*)

CHAPTER ONE

Two Wishes

Laurence was fed up with being a leprechaun.

He was tired of sitting under a boring old rainbow, guarding a mouldy old crock of gold and making endless shoes.

He wanted to be a human being.

And besides, he longed to have a Best Friend. But nobody is ever Best Friends with a leprechaun. Leprechauns spend all their time tricking people and laughing wickedly and stealing things and not letting people have their crocks of gold.

If he wanted to have a Best Friend, Laurence would have to REFORM HIS CHARACTER. But first, he had to get bigger. That was why, on this summer's morning, he was doing his stretching

exercises in the
sunshine. Regular
exercises would
surely bring him up to
the right height to
pass for a small
boy. And he was
practising his
English very
hard too.

The other leprechauns
jeered. 'You'll snap in the
middle one day,' they
growled, 'and that will be
the end of you.
Leprechauns aren't
supposed to be tall.
Anyway, what's

wrong with being a leprechaun?'

'It's too corny,' explained Laurence. 'It's just not cool. All the really hip people are huming beings.'

The others didn't agree.

'Well, name one hip person who's a leprechaun,' Laurence said. But of course they couldn't.

Laurence had marked out a watch-yourself-grow chart on a *buachallán*. He'd marked it in centimetres, because it's much more encouraging to watch yourself grow in centimetres than in inches.

He was just standing very still up against the stem of the *buachallán*, holding his breath and concentrating on being a centimetre taller, when a huge

shadow fell across the field.

Laurence shivered with cold. He wondered where the sun had gone. What could have happened?

He came out from under the *buachallán*, looked up towards the sky and straight into a pair of very large grey eyes, with long brown lashes, and pudgy pink cheeks under them.

Oops! He was cornered.

Now the one thing a leprechaun dreads is being spotted by a human being. It usually means having to cough up a crock of gold.

'Good morning.' Laurence grinned hopefully at the owner of the eyes.

'What's good about it?'

'I didn't say it *was* a good morning,' said Laurence. 'I just *wished* you one. It's not the same thing.'

'Humph,' said the fat girl sourly and sat down with a bump that made the

buachallán tremble. 'Anyway,' she went
on, 'leprechauns aren't supposed to say
Good morning. They're supposed to say
Top o' the mornin'.'

'*Raiméis!*' (This was Laurence's favourite word.) 'You've been reading too many silly books about leprechauns. And who says I'm a leprechaun?'

'Well, if you're not, you're a mighty strange-looking whatever-it-is-that-you're-supposed-to-be.'

'Well, I'm *not* a leprechaun,' said Laurence stoutly. 'I'm huming. Just like you.'

'Have it your own way. What's your name? Mine's Phoebe.'

'Phoebe!' said Laurence. '*Phoebe*! What sort of a name is that?'

'You shouldn't be rude about people's names,' said Phoebe primly. 'What's yours?'

'Laurence.'

Now, Laurence's name was really
Larry, but he thought that sounded too
leprechaunish altogether, so he'd
changed it to Laurence. That had a
definite human ring to it.

'Huh! That proves it!' said Phoebe.

'That proves what?'

'That you really *are* a leprechaun. All

leprechauns are called Laurence.'

'No, they're not. They're mostly called Larry, actually.'

'Same difference. Laurence is long for Larry.'

'What?'

'Or at least,' went on Phoebe thoughtfully, 'Larry is short for Laurence, which comes to the same thing. What age are you? I'm eleven.'

'Me too,' said Laurence. 'Eleven hundred next birthday.'

'Oh you big fibber!'

Big! She'd called him *big*! Laurence swelled up importantly. 'Am I?' he asked, delighted.

'Yes, of course you are. You must be fibbing, because nobody can live to be

eleven hundred. Unless ... unless ...
unless they're a *leprechaun*, of course.'

'But I'm not eleven hundred yet. Not
for another month. I'm still only one
thousand and ninety-nine.'

'And eleven months,' added Phoebe.
'Same difference though. You're way
too old to be a human being.'

'Well, OK, OK, perhaps I am a
leprechaun then,' Laurence admitted.
'But that doesn't mean I have a crock of
gold!'

Phoebe stretched out her plump legs.
'That's what they all say. Anyway, I
don't want your crummy old crock of
gold.'

Now Laurence had been brought up
to believe that human beings are always

on the lookout for crocks of gold. But here was his first-ever human being and she didn't want one!

'I'd much rather have three wishes,' Phoebe went on. 'Even one wish would do, actually. You don't happen to know any wishing-fairies, do you?'

Laurence shook his head. 'No such thing.'

'Are you sure? I thought that if there are leprechauns, there'd surely be wishing-fairies too.'

'No,' said Laurence firmly. 'At least, I

don't know any.'

'That's really too bad,' said Phoebe crossly. 'Can you do magic?'

'A bit,' said Laurence cautiously.

'What can you do?'

'I can disappear,' boasted Laurence.

'Well, that's not much use, is it?'

'I suppose not,' agreed Laurence sadly.

'Anything else?'

'No,' said Laurence in a small voice. 'Sorry. You make me sound quite useless.'

'Well, you are a bit. It's a shame you can't grant me any wishes. Have *you* got a wish?'

'Of course I have. I wish I wasn't a leprechaun. I wish I was taller. Tall enough to be a huming being.'

'Isn't it nice being a leprechaun?'

'No, it isn't. It's awful. But what's *your* dearest wish?' Laurence asked.

'Well,' began Phoebe, 'do you promise not to tell anyone else?'

'Cross my heart and hope to die.'

'Well, then,' Phoebe confided, 'I wish I was thin!'

'THIN!' exclaimed Laurence. 'THIN! What on earth do you want to be thin for?' That was the daftest wish he'd ever heard.

'They're all thinner than me at school,' said Phoebe.

'Probably,' said Laurence. 'But who cares about that? Who wants to be like everyone else?'

'You do, for a start,' said Phoebe. 'But

you see, the real problem is this. My big
sister wants me to be bridesmaid at her
wedding this summer, and I look so
stupid in frilly dresses! I look like ... I
look like ... a hippopotamus in a tutu!'

Laurence started to giggle. The giggle
turned into a chuckle.

The chuckle turned into a belly laugh,
and before long he was rolling around
on the grass with tears streaming down
his puckered old cheeks.

'A hippo ... a hoppo ... a
hoppopit ... a hippopot ...
a hippopotamus in a
tu ... in a tu ... in a
tutu!' he roared.

At last he sat up and took out
his handkerchief.

It was red with large white spots. He gave his nose a good blow.

'Oh just look at your hanky!' exclaimed Phoebe. Now it was her turn to giggle. 'It looks just like a handkerchief in a fairy-tale. It's a very *leprechaunish* sort of handkerchief!'

Laurence examined his hanky glumly. 'Now you see what I mean about being a leprechaun,' he said. 'People think I'm ridiculous. Or else they don't believe in me.'

'Who doesn't believe in you?'

'Oh, you know – people. Children nowadays are only interested in the ozone layer and computer games. Leprechauns are just too old-fashioned for them. And grown-ups gave up

believing in leprechauns years ago. It's
no fun being a leprechaun if you can't
annoy people. And you can't if they
don't believe in you. I mean, look at
you. You're not even interested in my
crock of gold.'

'But you said you hadn't *got* a crock of
gold,' said Phoebe.

'No. But if I had, you wouldn't want it
anyway. There's no fun in *not* giving
people your crock of gold if they don't
want it in the first place.'

'We're a right pair, aren't we?' said
Phoebe with a smile. 'You want to be
bigger, and I want to be smaller.'

Just then, Phoebe's brother called her
for her lunch. It was tuna-fish
sandwiches today, her very favourite,

and caramel pudding with cream to
follow, so she didn't want to be late.

'Look,' she whispered. 'Do you want

to sit here moping under this ragwort for the rest of your life, or would you like to come home with me?'

Laurence's heart gave a little jump. Go away with a human child! It sounded just the chance he needed to become part of the human world.

'Oh very well,' he said coolly, 'I haven't got anything special on today. I suppose I could give it a try.'

So Phoebe scooped him up and dropped him into her pocket, and ran off home to lunch.

Laurence settled in very nicely in Phoebe's room. At first, he wasn't too keen on her suggestion that he should live in her doll's house. He didn't like the idea of needing a specially small place for himself. He was still hoping to become a proper human being some day.

'There's always my sock drawer,' suggested Phoebe.

But Laurence kept getting lost in the sock drawer, and the fluff from the socks made him sneeze. So in the end he

had to settle for the doll's house after all.

'Don't tell anyone I'm here,' he warned Phoebe.

'What? You mean, it has to be a *secret*? But I want to show you to my friends. They've never met a leprechaun.'

'And they never will!' Laurence screamed, stamping his foot. 'Never! I'm not having a lot of humings staring at me and asking for my crock of gold. Never! Do you hear? *Never*! *Never*!'

Phoebe was startled. He really was a nasty little fellow. Should she send him back to the *buachallán* field right now? What was the point in having your own leprechaun if you couldn't show him off?

Still, it might be fun. Maybe she could

put up with his bad temper for a while anyway.

'Keep your hair on,' she said. 'Mum's the word.'

CHAPTER TWO

A Cool Dude

'I really must do something about my wardrobe,' said Laurence one day, after he had been living with Phoebe for about a week.

'What's wrong with it?' asked Phoebe, peering into the bedroom of the doll's house and opening the door of the tiny wardrobe.

'No, not that wardrobe, you *amadán*,' said Laurence. 'I mean my clothes.'

'Well, why didn't you say so?'

'I'm just practising using longer words in English,' Laurence explained. 'You know, I've had these clothes for three hundred years,' he went on. 'I think it's

really time I had some new ones. They're getting a bit tatty.'

'Green jacket, red cap, white owl's feather.' Phoebe looked him up and down. 'And pointy shoes with big shiny buckles. Very nice, but a bit on the shabby side, I agree. And perhaps just a teeny bit old-fashioned. But I haven't got any doll's clothes in your size, I'm afraid, and besides all my dolls are girls.'

'Good grief, you *amadán*, I don't want dolly clothes! Don't even think about it!' snapped Laurence.

Phoebe was stumped. She couldn't think of a single shop where they sold leprechaun-sized clothes. Maybe they could get some baby ones and wash and wash them and hope they shrank?

'No, no,' said Laurence grumpily. 'You don't *buy* leprechaun clothes. You make them.'

'But I can't sew!' wailed Phoebe.

'Who said anything about *you*?' said Laurence. 'I'll make them myself. Now, denim, I think, for the trousers. That's dead cool, isn't it? And maybe I'll have a denim jacket too. And a nice bit of colourful cotton for the shirt. Do you think you could manage that?'

'Please?' said Phoebe.

'*Please*,' added Laurence.

'All right so.'

Phoebe had a good rummage in her mother's ragbag and found a piece of red cotton for the shirt. Then she ripped the back pockets off an old pair of jeans.

That made two nice big pieces for the jacket and trousers.

'Are you sure you can sew?' she asked Laurence. Every time *she* tried sewing, she got blood all over the cloth because she pricked her fingers so often.

'Well, of course I can sew!' said Laurence crossly. 'What do you think leprechauns do all day?'

'I haven't a clue. Polish their gold, I suppose.'

Laurence thought this might be a trick to make him say that he had a crock of gold, so he ignored it. 'Why, we sew, of course,' he said. 'We sew shoes and boots. Look at my fine shoes. Where would you get a pair of shoes like that in a huming shop?'

'Oh, I forgot that leprechauns are cobblers. But if you can *all* make shoes, who buys them?'

'Nobody. We don't *sell* them. We just wear them. We all make our own shoes and wear them.'

'You spend all day making shoes for yourselves! But there must be thousands of pairs of leprechaun shoes. The countryside must be full of them.'

Phoebe was imagining mounds of
pointy buckled shoes all over the
country.

'It is, it is,' said Laurence proudly. 'We're the best shod people in Ireland, so we are. But you see, the thing is, we do a lot of dancing. At the crossroads, usually, or around a fairy ring.'

'Dancing! I didn't know you liked dancing.'

'Well, I don't like it actually. In fact, I *hate* it.'

'But why do you do it, then?'

'To wear out my shoes of course!' said Laurence, threading his needle. 'Now, go away and let me get on with my work.'

And before you could say jigs and reels, Laurence had made himself a brand new mega-cool suit.

And do you know what he looked like in it? Like a leprechaun in denims, that's what.

CHAPTER THREE

A Gremlin in the Works

'I'll never get the hang of this alphabet,' moaned Laurence, when Phoebe tried to teach him to read. 'The letters are such odd shapes.'

'No they're not,' said Phoebe. 'They're easy. *I've* been able to read since I was six.'

'I used to be quite good at Ogham when I was younger,' said Laurence. 'In fact, I was reading and

writing when I was about ninety. But that was much easier. All nice straight lines in places where you'd expect.'

'What's Ogham?' Phoebe asked.

'It's an ancient script we used to use in Ireland long ago.' And Laurence drew a few words in Ogham on her blackboard to show her.

'Hey, that's like a secret code!' said Phoebe. 'We could use it for private messages.'

'Only you can't write in English in it,'

warned Laurence. 'You'd better work harder at your Irish!'

'Yes, and you'd better work harder at learning to read ordinary writing,' said Phoebe.

And so he did. Before very long, Laurence was able to read whole sentences.

His favourite book was Phoebe's dictionary.

Phoebe explained to him that people don't actually *read* dictionaries; they just read a little bit about a single word when they want to know what it means.

Laurence thought this was a terrible waste. 'What about all the words you would never think of looking up? You might never find out about them at all!

No, no. That's a very bad way to use a dictionary,' he said. 'I'm going to start at the beginning and read it all right through to the end.'

So he started at the letter A and every day he read a page or two.

Before long, he had got to the letter G.

And there he found a word that *really* interested him.

'I think I've found myself a new career,' he announced to Phoebe that evening.

'Well?' said Phoebe. 'Go on. What is it?'

'Guess.'

'Hmm ... for a person such as yourself. For a very, very small person.'

'If you want to put it so unkindly, yes,' said Laurence haughtily. 'And of a certain character and background.'

'Let me see. An elf? A pixie? A gnome? That's it! You'd make quite a nice garden gnome, you know. You could sit by someone's pond all day and fish.'

'Don't be absurd, child,' said
Laurence. 'Garden gnomes are slightly
more awful even than leprechauns. No.

My new career is much more modern than that.'

'Well, what then? A TV announcer?'

'No. Guess again.'

'A waiter?' Phoebe was guessing wildly. 'A tax inspector? A bee-keeper? A fireman?'

'The bee-keeping idea isn't bad,' said Laurence. 'Maybe I'll keep that in reserve. But *I'm* going to be a *gremlin.*'

'A what?'

'A gremlin,' said Laurence. 'Isn't that a good idea?'

'Emm, is that something in Russia?' asked Phoebe.

'Russia? No. You can be a gremlin anywhere,' said Laurence. 'That's the beauty of it, you see.'

'I see,' said Phoebe, though in fact she didn't see at all. 'Do you need special training?'

'No. That won't be necessary,' said Laurence. 'Being a leprechaun for almost eleven hundred years should be enough. You see, to be a good gremlin you have to be as difficult, as awkward and as troublesome as possible. I think I have all the necessary skills.'

For once, Phoebe didn't argue. 'Oh, well,' she said, 'if it makes you happy, whatever it is ...'

The very next morning, Phoebe's father's alarm clock went off at four o'clock. It was still dark. But as he was very sleepy, Phoebe's father didn't even notice.

He stumbled out of bed, wriggled into his office clothes, knotted his beastly office tie, and went down to the kitchen to make breakfast.

Then he noticed that nobody else was up yet, so he went back to the foot of the stairs and yelled, 'Get up, you lazy things! Time for school!'

And so the whole family got up.

'How come it's still dark?' asked Phoebe's brother, as he ate his cornflakes.

'That's because it's so early,' said Phoebe's father looking at the kitchen clock. 'After all it's only . . . HALF PAST FOUR IN THE MORNING! Good grief! What happened to my alarm clock? Phoebe! Have you been messing with it again?' And her dad rushed out of the kitchen and up the stairs. Sure enough, the alarm was set for four o'clock.

'Don't you ever touch my clock again, Phoebe,' warned her father as they all went back to bed to snatch a few more hours of sleep.

'But I never . . . ' said Phoebe, yawning.

And that was only the start of it. Over the next few weeks, things went mysteriously wrong in Phoebe's household.

Her mother put some potatoes in the microwave one day, and came back to

find them smouldering and hissing.
When she took them out, one of them
actually burst into flames!

'Have you been fiddling with the
microwave, Phoebe?' asked her mother.
'Honestly, you're a fire hazard.'

'I didn't touch it!' said Phoebe.
'Why're you blaming me?'

Another day, Phoebe's brother turned

on his computer to play a game of chess, only to find that *all* the pieces were kings! All thirty-two of them! *'Phoe-be!'* he yelled.

'It wasn't me, it wasn't, it wasn't,' cried Phoebe. How come she was getting the blame for everything? That's what comes of being the youngest.

Now Phoebe was a smart kid, and it wasn't long before she began to realise that all these things had started to happen since Laurence had been around. Mischief. That's what leprechauns were good at.

This needed investigation! Phoebe marched to her bedroom and took her school dictionary off the bookshelf.

Laurence peered out of his doll's front

door. (He still hadn't grown much,
though he'd certainly got plumper since
he'd started sharing Phoebe's food.)

'What are you looking up?' he asked.

'Gremlin,' said Phoebe grimly. And
then she read out what it said:
*Mischievous sprite that interferes with
machines such as computers, telephones or
televisions, and makes them go mysteriously
wrong.*

'So it was you, Laurence. This is your famous career! You've been gremling around the house, haven't you, and *I've* been getting the blame.'

'*Me*?' said Laurence.

'Oh come on, Laurence, admit it.'

'Well, all right. I have. But wasn't it fun!' Laurence's eyes were shining. 'There you all were, having your breakfast at half past four in the morning! It was so funny! And you should have seen your brother's face when he tried . . . '

'*Laurence*!' snapped Phoebe. 'This just won't do. You've been getting me into heaps of trouble, and now you're making it worse by laughing! Oh, you are a nasty little ... a nasty little ... a nasty little *leprechaun*!'

'Ooh, don't say that, don't say that,' Laurence pleaded.

'I will,' said Phoebe. 'You're just not being fair.'

'Fair?' said Laurence, puzzled. 'What has that got to do with it?'

'Look, Laurence,' said Phoebe. 'You think being human has to do with size. Well, it hasn't. It has to do with things like playing fair and sticking by your friends and not getting other

people into trouble.'

'Has it?' asked Laurence in surprise.
'Are you sure?'

'Quite sure,' said Phoebe.

'Oh,' said Laurence, feeling extra
small all of a sudden. How was he ever
going to get to be human?

CHAPTER FOUR

A Golden Opportunity

'Where do you go when you disappear?'
Phoebe asked Laurence one day.

'Nowhere,' he said.

'But you must be somewhere,' she
argued.

'I'm *there* all right,' said Laurence. 'But
you can't see me.'

'You mean you're invisible?'

'No. *I* can see me, so I can't be
invisible. Disappearing has to do with
making people *believe* I'm not there.
Seeing is believing. Not believing is not
seeing.'

'Gosh,' said Phoebe. 'You make it
sound worse than grammar. And that's

the very worst thing. Except for long division of course. Long division is the very, very worst thing in the whole world.'

'Anyway, why do you want to know about disappearing?' asked Laurence.

'Well, I'd like to learn how to do it,' said Phoebe. 'Or at least how to partly do it.'

'What do you mean, partly?' asked Laurence.

'I want to make some of me disappear. There's too much of me, you see. If I could get rid of some of it, there'd be less.'

'Are we talking about being thin again?' asked Laurence.

'That's right,' said Phoebe.

'Have you tried dieting?'

'My mother says I'm too young to diet. I tell her I'm *big* enough, but she says it's not the same thing.'

'Oh, I don't mean serious dieting like eating only grapefruits for a month. I mean just not eating sticky buns and milkshakes and chocolate bars and

cherry log and chocolate mousse with whipped cream and slabs of toffee with roasted almonds in them and big fat chips with tomato ketchup and baked Alaska and sherry trifle and ice-cream sundaes and . . . '

'Of course I haven't,' said Phoebe. 'Life wouldn't be worth living!'

'How right you are!' said Laurence. 'You're a more sensible girl than you seem at times.'

'So will you teach me to disappear?' asked Phoebe.

'I don't think I can,' said Laurence. 'It's like being able to sing or being able to see colours. You either are or you're not. You can't learn it. If someone is tone-deaf or colour-blind, they just have to live with it.'

'Do you think it's something only leprechauns are able to do?'

'Yes, I think maybe that's it,' said Laurence.

'So being a leprechaun is quite useful sometimes?'

'I suppose so,' said Laurence reluctantly. 'But being huming is very nice too. Humings are cool.'

'Not fat ones,' said Phoebe sadly.

Laurence tactfully changed the subject. 'Let's get on with our Irish lessons,' he said.

But Phoebe wasn't listening. 'My Uncle Joe is coming to stay with us tomorrow,' she announced. 'He's American. What do you think of that?'

'A Murrican?' said Laurence. 'Hmm.'
Now I wonder, he thought to himself,
what kind of trick could I play on a
Murrican?

Uncle Joe arrived the next day. He
was very tall and thin, not a bit like a
normal American.
But he did have
three suitcases,
check trousers
and a very
loud voice.

'You're just cute, honey,' he said to Phoebe, pinching her plump cheeks.

Nobody had ever called Phoebe cute before. She wasn't sure if she liked it.

Now, Uncle Joe is a very nice man, I am sure. But he did wear everyone out. He wanted to buy lots of green cardigans and jumpers, because he thought that was what you did in Ireland.

'We wear other colours too,' Phoebe tried explaining to him.

'Yes, but real Irish sweaters are green,' insisted Uncle Joe.

'Well, Aran sweaters aren't,' said Phoebe. 'They're made of *báinín*, which actually means white.'

Uncle Joe didn't seem to understand.

He asked
Phoebe to
show him some
shamrock.

'We only have
it on St Patrick's
day,' said Phoebe. 'The rest of the year
we have roses and lilies and carnations
and delphiniums like everyone else.'

Uncle Joe was disappointed. 'I
suppose the next thing you'll say is that
you have no leprechauns either.'

'Oh no,' said Phoebe, pleased to be able to give him some good news. 'We have *those* all right.'

'Hey!' said Uncle Joe. 'Have you ever actually seen one?'

'Of course I have,' said Phoebe coolly.

'Go on!' said Uncle Joe. 'A real live leprechaun? Did you get his crock of gold?'

'Oh, that's only a story. They don't have any gold,' said Phoebe.

'Did the leprechaun tell you that?'

'Yes.'

'Well, he would, wouldn't he?' said Uncle Joe.

'But this leprechaun is different!' said Phoebe. 'This leprechaun is my Best Friend.'

When Laurence heard this (he was hiding in Phoebe's pocket), he got a very strange feeling all up his back. He was somebody's Best Friend, and he hadn't even tried to be!

'Oh, go on!' said Uncle Joe again. 'I don't believe a word of it!' And he gave a very loud laugh.

'He is, he *is*,' insisted Phoebe tearfully.

Laurence, inside her pocket, was beginning to get worried. Was she going to fish him out? And sure enough, before you could say begobs and begorrah, Phoebe had grabbed him by the feet and yanked him out of her pocket.

Quick as a flash, Laurence disappeared.

'Look!' exclaimed Phoebe, waving
Laurence at Uncle Joe.

'Look at what?' asked Uncle Joe,
for of course he could see nothing.

'Oh!' said Phoebe, looking at her
fingers and realising there was nothing

there. 'He must have disappeared!'

And she burst into tears, partly because she was disappointed that she couldn't show off her leprechaun to her uncle, and partly because she realised that she really shouldn't have tried to produce Laurence without his permission.

Now when Laurence heard how upset Phoebe sounded, he made a very brave decision. She was his Best Friend after all. He reappeared, right there in front of Uncle Joe's eyes!

'Hey!' said Uncle Joe, amazed. 'But he's wearing denims! He can't be a proper leprechaun.'

'Well, you're wearing a tam o'shanter,' said Laurence. 'You can't be

a proper Murrican.'

'This?' said Uncle Joe, feeling his head. 'This is my Irish cap.'

'*Raiméis*,' said Laurence. 'Everyone knows those are Scottish!'

'Oh really, are they?' said Uncle Joe, so concerned about his headgear that he forgot to be surprised that he was having a conversation with a leprechaun.

Well, the long and the short of it was that Uncle Joe wanted to take Laurence back to America with him.

'You'd have a wonderful time,' he assured Laurence. 'You'd be famous, a celebrity. You'd be a TV star. Coast-to-coast. You might even get a part in a movie. Oh my, it would be splendid. You could have a brilliant career.'

'Go on, go on!' said Laurence eagerly. 'I'd be famous, would I?'

'Oh yes, indeed. The country would go wild for you. They might even want to make you president! A real Irish leprechaun. *Unbelievable*!'

Laurence came down to earth with a bang. 'Unbelievable? I'd be unbelievable, would I?'

'Oh, absolutely,' agreed Uncle Joe eagerly.

'Well, thank you very much, your honour,' said Laurence, giving a stiff little bow. 'But you know, I can be unbelievable right here in Ireland.'

And with that, he sat down comfortably in Phoebe's hand and

closed his eyes, and politely but firmly refused to have anything more to do with the conversation.

CHAPTER FIVE

A Happy Ending

'I'm so sorry for showing you off to Uncle Joe,' said Phoebe to Laurence later. 'I know I shouldn't have done it without asking you first. You were a real friend to un-disappear yourself like that, and not leave me looking like a right eejit.'

'Well, you *were* a right eejit,' said Laurence, 'but I couldn't disgrace you like that in front of that Murrican, now could I? After all, we're Best Friends, aren't we?'

'Why did you decide not to go to America?' asked Phoebe. 'It sounded like you could have a great time.'

'Well,' said Laurence. 'I don't think I

would like to be a media leprechaun. I'd have to be even more leprechaunish than ever, for a start. And I've been going to such trouble to be *less* like a leprechaun. And then, of course, I have a Best Friend here in Ireland.'

'You know, Laurence,' said Phoebe, 'you're a very nice leprechaun, really, if you don't mind my saying so.'

'I don't,' said Laurence. 'And I see now that I'm never going to be anything else but a leprechaun. I can't seem to grow at all, and there's no point in trying to be a huming being, just to be cool. There are lots of very uncool huming beings.'

'Like Uncle Joe,' laughed Phoebe. 'And Laurence, have you noticed how *thin* Uncle Joe is? Thin, but not very hip.'

Laurence nodded. That was just what he thought.

'Oh Laurence,' went on Phoebe, 'wait till you see the fabulous outfit my sister has got me for the wedding. Velvet trousers and a jacket and a big floppy hat. No frills at all! I'm going to look great.'

And she did. Perfectly splendid. Not in the least like a hippopotamus. And Laurence sewed on some new buttons for her that made her outfit look even more splendid still.

And they went on being Best Friends for a very long time indeed. Laurence never went back to live with the leprechauns, but he was quite happy to

be a leprechaun in the human world, as long as they didn't put him on the television. And in time, he became quite a human sort of leprechaun.

Oh yes, and Laurence finally admitted to Phoebe that he really *did* have a crock of gold, and they were able to use some of it to have a nice holiday and buy some presents for Phoebe's family, and still have some left over for Phoebe to live on when she grew up.

OTHER BOOKS FROM
THE O'BRIEN PRESS

WOODLAND FRIENDS SERIES:

THE HEDGEHOG'S PRICKLY PROBLEM
Don Conroy

Harry hedgehog joins the circus to find adventure but ends up in a very prickly situation!

Paperback £3.99

THE TIGER WHO WAS A ROARING SUCCESS
Don Conroy

A large orange stranger turns up in the woodlands and causes havoc – and some fun!

Paperback £3.99

THE OWL WHO COULDN'T GIVE A HOOT
Don Conroy

All owls can hoot, can't they? But not Barny. The woodland friends try to solve the problem – but is it really a problem at all?

Paperback £3.99

THE BAT WHO WAS ALL IN A FLAP
Don Conroy

A flying fox causes quite a stir in the woodland, but it's really Lenny the bat, far away from his home in Australia.

Paperback £3.99

CARTOON FUN
Don Conroy

Draw your own cartoons and get excellent results – super heroes, animals, people, faces, comic strips, monsters, dinosaurs, birds. Easy-to-follow instructions and great fun. It *really* works!

Paperback £4.99

WILDLIFE FUN
Don Conroy

How to create lively and true-to-life drawings as well as cartoon animals. Failsafe instructions and models to follow. Includes lots of information on the lives of the animals. Full of fascinating fun.

Paperback £4.99

THE LOUGH NEAGH MONSTER
Sam McBratney
Illus. Donald Teskey

When NESSIE arrives from Scotland to visit her monster cousin NOBLETT there is bound to be trouble. Noblett loves his peaceful secret garden and has little time for his troublesome cousin from Loch Ness.

Paperback £3.99

THE KING'S SECRET
Patricia Forde

King Lowry Lynch has a terrible secret. He has the ears of a horse, and no one must find out. Especially his mother, Queenie. The traditional story of Lowry Lynch is now retold in an up-to-date, wacky new style that will appeal to even the most modern young readers.

Paperback £3.99

ART, YOU'RE MAGIC!
Sam McBratney

Arthur Smith wants to be liked. Everyone is nice to Mervyn Magee when he comes to school wearing a blue bow-tie like a butterfly - even Henrietta Turtle. So Art decides he needs a butterfly tie too. It's not popularity he gets though, but trouble – lots of it!

Paperback £3.50

THE FIVE HUNDRED
Eilís Dillon

Luca, an ambitious antique dealer, buys his heart's desire – a Fiat 500. When his car is stolen, life becomes dangerously exciting!

Paperback £3.95

Send for our full colour catalogue